This book is dedicated to my
daughter, Memphis Love Kinberg,
and her father, Simon.
You two have forever changed
my life and my heart.

A FEIWEL AND FRIENDS BOOK
An imprint of Macmillan Publishing Group, LLC
120 Broadway, New York, NY 10271
mackids.com

Our books may be purchased in bulk for promotional, educational, or business use.
Please contact your local bookseller or the Macmillan Corporate and Premium Sales Department
at (800) 221-7945 ext. 5442 or by email at MacmillanSpecialMarkets@macmillan.com.

Library of Congress Cataloging-in-Publication Data is available.
ISBN 978-1-250-26949-2 (hardcover) / ISBN 978-1-250-81040-3 (special edition)

First edition, 2021
Book design by Mike Burroughs
Feiwel and Friends logo designed by Filomena Tuosto

All illustrations were created using watercolor and ink.

Printed in the United States of America by Phoenix Color, Hagerstown, Maryland

3 5 7 9 10 8 6 4

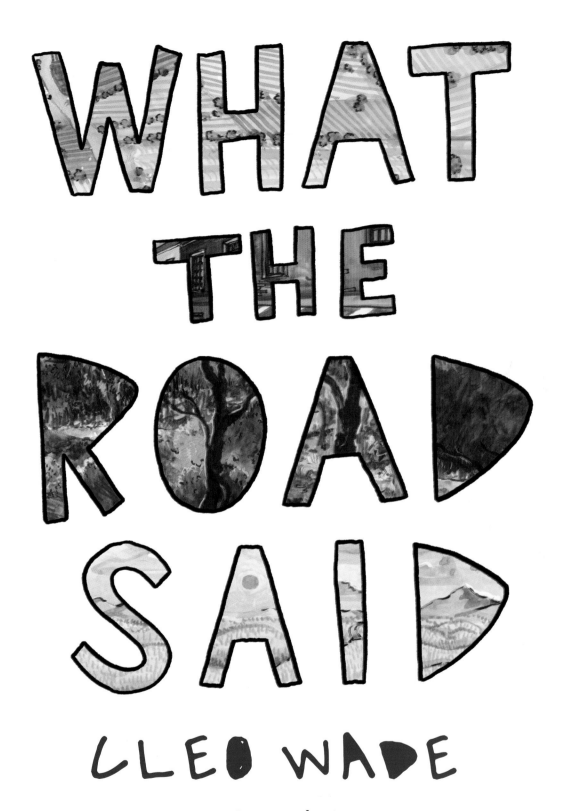

WHAT THE ROAD SAID

CLEO WADE

ILLUSTRATED BY **Lucie de Moyencourt**

Feiwel and Friends
New York

Have you ever wanted to go
in a different direction?

Have you ever wondered if there was
something more . . .
something out there . . .
something just . . .
different?

I did too.

Then one day I was walking my usual way home
when,
out of nowhere,
for no reason at all,
almost as if it were magic,
a road appeared.
I could not believe my eyes,
so I walked over to it and . . .

I said to the road,

WHERE DO YOU LEAD?

The Road said,
Be a leader and find out.

HOW DO I START?

I asked.

The Road smiled and said,
You have already started.

WELL, WHAT HAPPENS WHEN I GET THERE?

We have just begun! said the Road.
Do not skip straight to the ending.
Enjoy the beginning and the middle too.

WHICH WAY DO I GO?

That is your choice to make,
said the Road.

BUT WHAT IF I GO THE WRONG WAY?

The Road curved a little, almost as if it was giving me a hug, and said, Do not worry. Sometimes we go the wrong way on our way to the right way.

WHAT IF I GET SCARED?

That is okay. You are brave,
said the Road.

BUT WHAT DOES IT
MEAN TO BE BRAVE?

I asked.

The Road guided me through a very gloomy forest.
Even though I was frightened, I trusted the Road,
and as I took one step, and then another step
after that, the Road gently whispered,

Being brave is when you are afraid of
doing something, but you do it anyway.
Do not let what scares you keep you
from continuing on your path . . .

WILL I ALWAYS
MOVE FORWARD?

Not always, said the Road.

WHY NOT?

Because sometimes you
will stumble backward and
sometimes you will stand still.

WHAT IF I **FALL?**

Everyone falls at some point, said the Road.
But I will always be there when you land.

WHAT IF I GET LOST?

There may be some days that feel long and dark,
said the Road, but I promise that, no matter what, I will give
you the evening stars and morning sun to light your way.

WHAT IF I GROW WEARY OR GET HURT?

I will give you trees of all shapes and sizes to shelter you when you need to rest and heal, said the Road.

You are never alone,
said the Road.

WHAT IF I CHANGE?

Come with me, said the Road.

And as I moved forward
the Road introduced me to a
caterpillar and a family of seeds.

We did not stay long.
The Road began taking me on a
journey through the seasons.

I watched summer turn to fall, and fall turn to
winter, and as spring was upon us, I realized
we had gone in one big beautiful circle.

I looked down and found I was standing in front
of the caterpillar and the seeds once more.

Only the caterpillar was no longer a caterpillar
and the seeds had turned to flowers of every color,
swaying in the sun.

The Road then raised me up and said,
All things grow and change. That is the
magic of being alive. You, too, will find your
wings. You, too, will bloom. No living thing
is meant to stay the same.

WHAT IF I NEED HELP ON MY JOURNEY?

Ask your fellow travelers along the way.

WHAT IF THEY ARE
MEAN TO ME?

Lead them to kindness, said the Road.

HOW?

By being kind.

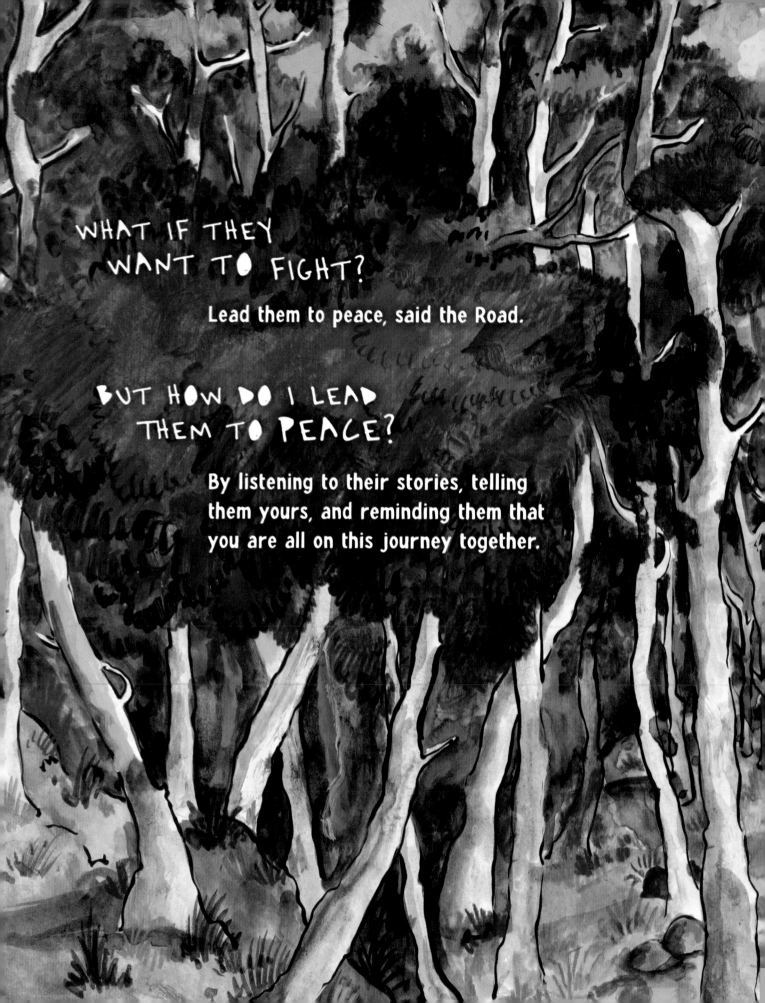

WHAT IF THEY
WANT TO FIGHT?

Lead them to peace, said the Road.

BUT HOW DO I LEAD
THEM TO PEACE?

By listening to their stories, telling
them yours, and reminding them that
you are all on this journey together.

WHAT IF THE
WORLD AROUND US
IS FILLED WITH HATE?

Lead it to love.

HOW?

By sharing the power of your love with it,
said the Road.

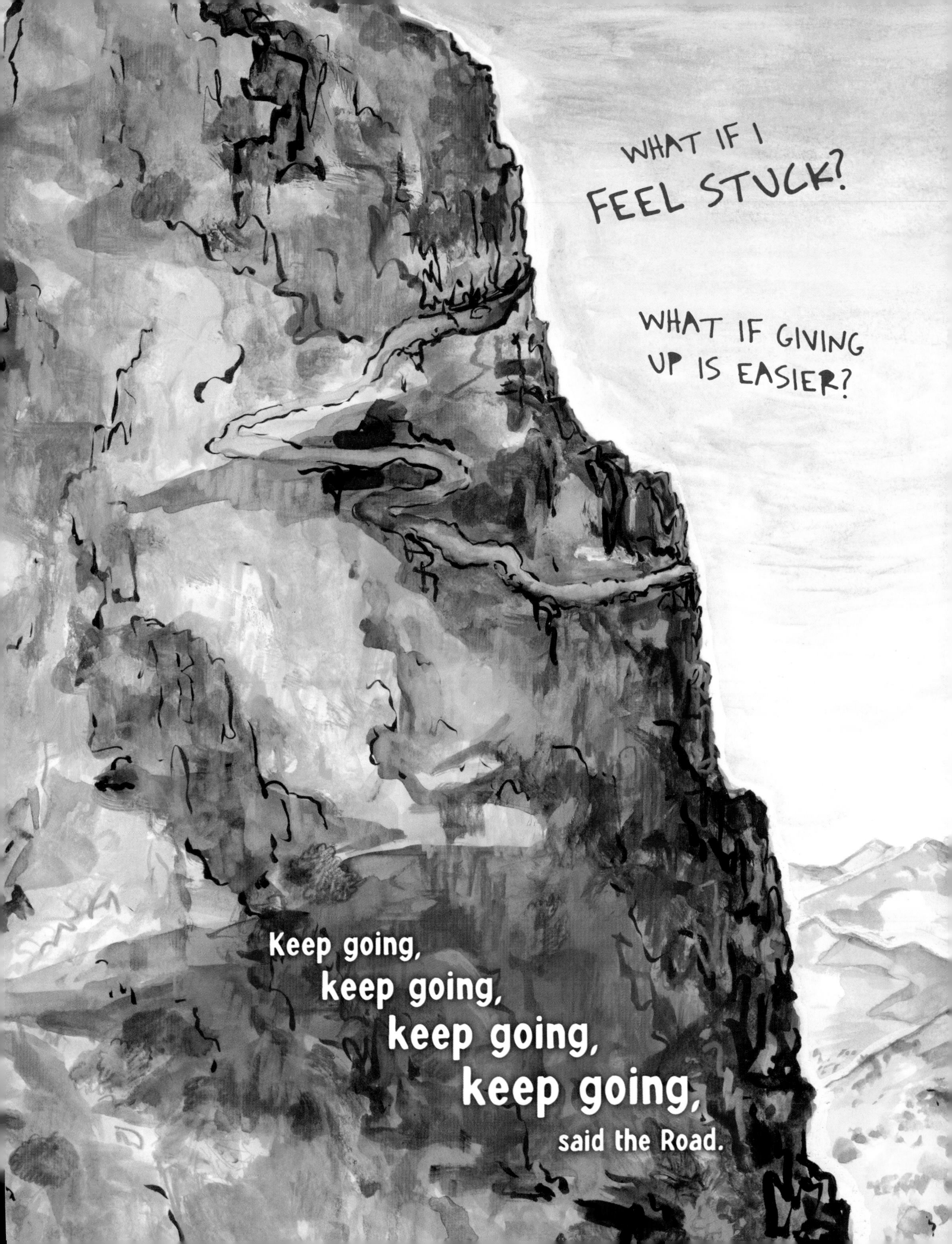

Keep going,
keep going,
keep going,
keep going,
said the Road.

WHAT IF I CAN'T DO IT?

You can, said the Road.

HOW DO YOU KNOW?

Because you
have come this far,
said the Road.

The Road said,
BE A LEADER AND FIND OUT.

AUTHOR'S NOTE

Dearest you,

I wrote this book in hopes that the Road can be your friend through every stage of your journey. I hope you will allow it to live with you in the world as a hug on your good days and also on the days when you might feel alone, or scared, or confused by big questions. I wrote these words to encourage you, love you, and help you on your path to becoming who you are. You are important, you are here on purpose, and you deserve to be the leader of your life.

This is a book for children (I really needed this book as a child). But this is also a book for adults (being a grown-up is hard and the Road reminds me to take it one day at time).

From my heart to yours, this book is for you.

Love,
CLEO